TOY SOLDIERS

A SHORT STORY

ALEXANDRIA BLAELOCK

BlueMere Books
MELBOURNE, AUSTRALIA

For permission requests, please contact
enquiries@bluemerebooks.com.

Ordering Information:
Discounts are available on quantity purchases. For details, contact orders@bluemerebooks.com.

Toy Soldiers/Alexandria Blaelock
paperback ISBN: 978-1-925749-41-0
digital ISBN: 978-1-925749-42-7

Book Layout © BookDesignTemplates.com

TOY SOLDIERS

Mikke squinted, but his eyes refused to focus.

He blinked a couple of times, but they didn't clear, so he rubbed them with the knuckles of his index fingers.

His eyes were dry and scratchy, and rubbing them with his dirty fingers just added pain to the mix.

Not that there was much to see past the piles of rubble. The moon was hiding behind the clouds as if it was afraid too.

His body felt so heavy, he could barely stand upright - not even buoyed by the emptiness of his stomach.

He settled his back on the bombed-out wall behind him and closed his eyes for a second just to rest them.

And woke up when his chin hit his chest.

It wasn't really any wonder, he was only twelve.

Before The War, he'd be tucked up in bed, warm and sleepy, on a full stomach after a big cuddle from Mummy by this time.

Not filthy, tired and hungry. And not exactly sure where Mummy was.

But his country was depending on him, so he did what was expected.

He kept watch for the enemy, hoping all the while he didn't have to do anything more than run and tell the grown-ups.

He put up a brave face and talked big with the other boys, but he was very afraid there would be fighting, and he might get hurt.

Possibly even more frightening, that he might have to hurt someone else before The War was over.

He could hardly remember a time before The War, a time before fear became his constant companion.

Though he seemed to recall a house with intact walls and a smooth flat garden with scented flowers. There was Mummy and Papa. And there were cuddles, food and warmth.

He was fairly sure there was a soft teddy and a toy car.

And a warm, snuggly purring cat.

He was sorry he'd been in such a hurry to grow up.

To prove he was a man.

It's true - you should be careful what you wish for.

He crouched and picked at a scab on his knee as he strained to hear what was out there.

But aside from the distant bombing, slates sliding off what was left of the roofs into what was left of the houses, and the rattle of gunfire, there didn't seem to be anything else.

He hissed as the dried blood gave way and tore open the new skin.

A drop of bright red blood bloomed in the dirt.

The townsfolk were quiet - assuming there were any left.

And there were no birds, no foxes, no rabbits, and no rats either.

No night time insects chirping in the darkness.

Nothing, except somewhere out there, another sleepy boy or ten.

Who wanted nothing more to be safe at home.

It was only the big boys, full of raging teenage hormones that still wanted to be out on the front lines.

One time, maybe a hundred years ago, he'd been out riding his bike with Mummy, and they'd passed two troop trucks.

One going out with young, fresh-faced boys - fists pumping, whooping and hollering.

The other coming back with silent, dishevelled men, who sat with heads bowed, their bodies held upright by the guns they were leaning on.

A bit like Mikke now, only without the gun.

He forgot where he was for a moment, and took a deep breath to sigh out, choking on dust and the smell of dead things.

He pulled his torn and threadbare coat tighter around his shoulders, but it didn't do much for the chill in the air.

Though his teeth could have been chattering as much from fear as from the cold.

He heard something scrabbling across the rubble, and terror struck him rigid.

He didn't know if it was a man or an animal, but he knew he wanted to run away.

Though he couldn't make his legs move.

Now he knew what rabbits felt like, and there wasn't even a headlight.

All he could do was hope he looked like a vaguely human-shaped pile of brick rubble in the shadows.

"Mikke," someone whispered loudly, "Mikke."

Oh, thank God. It was Anton.

"Here," he whispered back.

Anton scrabbled a little further and plopped down beside him.

"You shouldn't be here," said Mikke.

"I know," Anton said, pausing to rub some more dirt on his glasses in the hope of taking some off, "but I was bored, and a bit lonely."

"Me too."

They giggled at each other, and for an instant, it was almost like before The War when they used to sneak down to the brook to catch tadpoles.

And tell each other stories about the beautiful Angelika, who was two years older than them, and whom they both wanted to marry.

When the worst of their concerns was getting covered in mud and being late for dinner.

And that Angelika might prefer Dietrich who was the same age as her, and whose name sounded better next to hers.

Then a bomb went off somewhere, and the sky went red, and after a bit, they heard the roar and felt the boom thump into their bodies along with some bricks shaken loose from the wall.

Mikke sighed, and coughed, again, "I wish things were different."

"I know."

Anton scratched his left arm, the one his jacket was missing, the one gashed open and almost certainly infected by now. "I keep wondering how I got from wrestling and hiking in the forest with the Youth Club to here, now. Waiting for the enemy to attack."

"I don't know. It doesn't make any sense."

"I don't remember choosing this."

"We didn't choose this," Mikke waved his arm to include the bombed-out landscape, "but we did choose to join the club. It was like a gang, only better."

Anton nodded, "I suppose when you put it like that…"

For a moment they slumped, lost in memories of the first few heady days. The games and competitions, the shouting, the feeling of becoming something more than yourself.

Anton sat up, "hey, did I tell you I saw Angelika at the market the other day?"

"No, what happened?"

"She smiled at me."

"Was it a smile because she knows you, or a smile because she likes you?"

"Definitely because she likes me."

They laughed.

"I don't know Mikke, she looked different. Like a grown-up."

"Was she wearing lipstick or something?"

"Probably, and she did something different with her hair; tied it up on the back of her head instead of in pigtails down the side."

"Beautiful."

They were silent a few moments as they imagined her.

"What was she wearing?" Mikke asked.

"Black. A suit of some kind."

"Did she sign up?"

"Wouldn't she be too young?"

"Aren't we? Yet look at us sitting here."

"But she's just a girl!"

"I'm pretty sure she's not just anything. I wouldn't want to try my luck against hers."

"'Spose not."

They sat quietly, wondering about grown-up Angelika.

"So, what were you doing at the market?"

"What?"

"At the market Anton, what were you doing at the market?"

"Oh yeah. I went to headquarters to check-in for reassignment, but there was no one there."

"What, no one at all?"

"No one."

"I wonder where they all went."

"Ernst told me the order came for a final assault."

Mikke laughed, "but if Ernst was there, there was someone there."

"He was just leaving. But he told me the order came for a final assault."

"Final assault?"

"Yes, Mikke, final."

"But then what?"

"I don't know. What comes after final?"

"Well, nothing comes after final. Final is the last one."

"And what are we supposed to do Anton?"

"I don't know, he didn't say."

"So they're making the final assault, and we're... What? Going with them or waiting for them to come back?"

"See? That's why I came looking for you. You always understand this kind of thing."

Mikke frowned and scratched his head, "what do you think will happen after The War?"

"Won't everything go back to the way it was?"

"But how can it?"

"I don't know, but how can it not?"

"You can't change what's already happened."

"I mean that we'll just go back to school, and Miss Wagner will shout at us when we get our spelling wrong, and we'll play chasey in the yard with the other boys and come home to do the chores and all that."

"Um, yes, but, well, Miss Wagner's dead and so are Otto, Mathie and Karl."

"No! When did that happen Mikke?"

"A couple of weeks ago when there was that truck crash."

"That's terrible, I didn't know. I don't know what to say about that."

"I feel like there's just been too much of that kind of thing, and I can't see any way past it."

"But—"

"I don't see how I can go back to school Anton, or even be normal again after all this."

"But Mikke—"

"I can't even imagine being happy again."

"Don't say that Mikke, Mummy says—"

"I'm so tired of this. You can have Angelika, but you have to promise me you'll make her happy. That you'll be happy."

Anton struggled to his knees and threw his scrawny arms around Mikke, "don't talk like that Mikke. Mummy says it's always darkest before dawn. We don't have to work it all out right now. All we have to do is survive until morning, and then we can think about it again."

Mikke laid his forehead on his friend's shoulder and cried.

Not the shrill blubbing of a boy over a trifle, but the harsh, gut-wrenching sobs of a man who can't see anything to live for.

"It's going to be all right," Anton said, patting his back, "one way or another, it's going to work out."

"I wish I had your confidence."

"Yes, well I've seen the alternative, and I don't recommend it."

"I forgot. I'm sorry about your Dad."

"See, that's the thing Mikke, you just have to keep moving forward. It's the easiest thing, and at the same time, it's the hardest thing."

Mikke sat up and wiped his nose on his sleeve.

He was about to reply when a bomb went off somewhere closer, and they lost their footing and fell.

At the end of the street, the Post Office erupted in a ball of hot light. Mikke was transfixed by the spectacle. It was like a book burning times ten million.

The flames roasted the sky; he felt their warmth on his face, and couldn't look away.

Anton hauled him upright and tried to drag him clear.

Mikke wrestled his way free and took a step towards the fire. It would be so easy to end all this fear and doubt.

All he had to do was walk into the fire, and it would be over.

Anton shouted something he couldn't hear and pulled his arm, trying to drag him back again.

Mikke shrugged him off and took another step toward the fire.

But Anton wasn't having any of it.

He launched himself at Mikke, knocking him back down to the ground, and settling himself on Mikke's guts.

He started shouting incoherently as he pounded Mikke's chest with his clenched fists. Tears streamed down his face.

Mikke couldn't hear anything over the roar in his ears, but he looked up at Anton's screwed up face dripping tears down onto his own, and wondered if that was what happened.

You just kept going for the Antons of the world, the ones who had some kind of vision for the future, but needed someone stable to hold them up and push them forward.

Anton who'd already lost much more than him, but was somehow still leading the way.

He grabbed Anton's wrists and smiled up at him.

"We should probably find somewhere safer than this to wait for the dawn."

Anton slumped on his chest like the eleven-year-old baby he was, and Mikke patted his back.

Even though he didn't see a future for himself, it was enough for him to be the person Anton needed.

THE END

ABOUT THE AUTHOR

Alexandria Blaelock writes stories, some of them for *Ellery Queen's Mystery Magazine* and *Pulphouse Fiction Magazine*. She's also written four self-help books applying business techniques to personal matters like getting dressed, cleaning house, and feeding your friends.

As a recovering Project Manager, she's probably too fond of sticking to plan. She lives in a forest because she enjoys birdsong, the scent of gum leaves and the sun on her face. When not telecommuting to parallel universes from her Melbourne based imagination, she watches K-dramas, talks to animals, and drinks Campari. At the same time.

Discover more at www.alexandriablaelock.com.

Alma's Grace
Balancing the Book
Bygone Boyfriend
Carmelita Basingstoke
Fate in Your Hands
Kiss of Death
Lady of the Looking Glass
Life in the Security Directorate
Long Weekend in the Snow
Love in the Security Directorate
Morning Star, Evening Star, Superstar
Needy Bitch
Payton's Run
Phoenix Child
Secret Singer
Shining Star
Ship in a Bottle
Simone Says Hands in the Air
The Day the Schedule Broke
The Guardian's Vigil
Toy Soldiers

BOOKS BY ALEXANDRIA BLAELOCK

FICTION

That Love Nonsense

MS BLAELOCK'S BOOKS

Stress Free Dinner Parties
Signature Wardrobe Planning
Holistic Personal Finance
Minimally Viable Housekeeping